Encounters

Genna —
Hope you never
meet any of these
men!

J Crygle

Encounters

A Novel

Jean L. Croyle, former dating guru and contributor to several non-fiction publications.

iUniverse, Inc.
New York Bloomington

Encounters

This is a work of fiction. All of the characters, names, incidents, organizations, and dialogue in this novel are either the products of the author's imagination or are used fictitiously.

iUniverse books may be ordered through booksellers or by contacting:

iUniverse
1663 Liberty Drive
Bloomington, IN 47403
www.iuniverse.com
1-800-Authors (1-800-288-4677)

ISBN: 978-0-595-51068-9 (pbk)
ISBN: 978-0-595-61754-8 (ebk)

Printed in the United States of America

Dedication

ENCOUNTERS is written for so many but dedicated to only one-the author's mom, Beatrice Levine, who offered sage advice, a generous heart, and always, always support of her daughter. Thanks, Mom.

Prologue

We have read them on tee shirts, coffee mugs, and bumper stickers; some have memorized the saying: 'so many men, so little time'. Single women have been both encouraged and disheartened by this catchy little slogan. We have dated and shared quality (?) time with people whose exact qualities remains an enigma long after the meeting itself. These people may include former spouses, new friends, arranged dates, friends of friends, and even some we work with or have seen on the elevator. We peer at each with an eye toward the future (husband material?). We imagine introducing him into the eager-for-us-to-settle-down family; we think of him in the morning's harsh light—*will he still be cute with bed-head?* Obsessed with the habits, language, manners and generosity factor, we rate them on imaginary scales in our ever-processing minds. I, Tessa Schaefer, am waiting for that man, and have been for a long, long time.

We have creatively used the Personal Ads in order to meet the man of our dreams (as someone once told me, "he doesn't have to be Mr. Right … just Mr. Right *Now*.") We are 'scoping' out the field for the man who will be passionate, realistic, good to his mom and attractive. We place ads with cutesy sayings such as "city smart, country heart," or "peppy, plump and pleasing," or using initials because space costs money, such as SWFNK. (Translated that means Single White Female No Kids). It is all done in the name of the goal: finding the husband.

For several years, these 'encounters' cried out for public attention. Some were revolting, a few enchanting, and many others either amused or simply entertained. With the advancement of the Internet, the Personal Ads took on a more aggressive stance: now you can view your prospective date, and even rule them out without sharing one minute of your time

1

with them. Who knows if this is progress? It is happening; people are logging on and continuing their search for the ideal mate.

So, kick off your shoes, adjust the pillow and be prepared to step into the world of Tessa's ENCOUNTERS. You may feel a kinship with her and in this private setting, you may enjoy some hearty laughs and heavy sighs. And that's good.

Coconut Joe

Looking into the highly lighted mirror, I decided that I was looking quite pretty, maybe lovely even. Big green eyes, apt nose, clear skin and perfect teeth (thanks to Mom, Dad and the heavy-handed orthodontist of my childhood). Curly dark hair (dark ash brown, the label said) styled by Rudy and makeup suited for a businesswoman completed the picture. A slight double chin, but hey! Can't be perfect, after all. My date for this evening, Joe, had told me he liked women with meat on their bones and I guess that includes some on their neck too. He admitted he was no Adonis, what with some pounds he didn't need and being near-sighted. The last date had been very handsome but had sour breath, poor posture and left a cheap tip. The posture and the breath could be fixed. The tip part—good riddance.

Back to Joe. Came from the suburbs, was an insurance adjuster, had a dream of winning the lottery so as to set up animal refuge havens and had a sweet tooth for candy. Sounded quite sweet and generous, and any-one who liked chocolate was already on my good side. He stated he was looking for a "special" kind of girl and he would tell me more about that when we'd met. I thought about that. I was special—didn't Dad say so? He said I was as beautiful as Snow White herself-was that special enough, I wondered. Joe had hesitated before agreeing to meet and I had asked him about that. Joe admitted to being uptight about seeing one another. Seemed his last date through the Personal Ads was blind. Legally. And she hadn't had the courtesy of telling him beforehand, leaving him unnerved and pitying. Joe insisted that he wouldn't have minded her being blind if she had been honest with him. I rolled my eyes, mentally calling him a liar, but hey, there are some folks out there, men included, who see beyond the scope of outer beauty. Hopefully he was one of them.

The pink sweater and tan slacks looked feminine and I selected a lightweight jacket for our spring time date. Big-haired, full-figured and all woman, that's what he was getting with this package, so said the mirror. Always surprised by women's magazines that have numerous articles about learning to love yourself, I realized that for me, that's a natural state. When I was little and thought no one was watching, I would gaze and speak to the mirror, imitating movie stars and imagining that I looked like a cross between Liz Taylor and Miss America. No, loving myself came by naturally, faults and all, and I just hoped that Joe's flaws were as simple to live with as mine were. I heard the buzzer, indicating my date was here, so I took a deep breath, three exactly, and went to meet the man.

Joe was tall, well over six feet, with standard glasses and a build I label 'stocky.' He had a pleasant demeanor, and looked like he approved of me too. Going well already, the inner self sang. He had a nervous grin, was overdressed for the balmy weather and offered a firm, somewhat soggy, handshake. Light cologne wafted from him as he toured my apartment and complimented me on a collage of dogs and cats I fancied. He declined a cold drink and seemed eager to go out on our date. Two points for Joe, for not making any smart remarks about being alone in the apartment with "the girl of my dreams" routine.

His car, a Buick something, was fairly clean except for two candy wrappers that slid gracefully to the floor. He tried to whisk them away before I noticed, which was cute. A choco-holic in our midst? That would make two of us, I gleefully thought. Joe spoke candidly about the perils of dating through the Personal Ads and repeated the story about the blind "chick." Not that it mattered, he insisted. I didn't respond. Why challenge him now? His car, my life in his hands … not a good time to make waves. He told me I was "one good looking lady, is the word 'lady' acceptable nowadays?" I nodded and approved of him trying his best to be nice.

Over a light supper I noted beads of sweat around Joe's forehead and down the sides of his face. Surely the jacket over the sweater over the longsleeved shirt was a bit much. Joe disagreed, "It's our first date and I believe in lookin' proper." Weird, my outer self warned. I would have preferred less proper and less sweat.

We shared a few laughs and he admitted to eating three candy bars on the way to my home—from nerves, he said. I decided to ask him what "special" meant to him when he used that term in our telephone discussion. What would make a date special? As if by rote, he responded,

"That she be honest and accept me 'as is' without hesitation," he finished. As is? As in buying a used car or piece of furniture? Usually that means with the problems—what problems? What would be the malfunction? I thought of myself as the consumer and remembered: Buyer Beware!

Later, lingering for a moment at my front door (very old fashioned and quite nice), he kissed me good night, and his one simple kiss was lightly refreshing. He was sweet and sincere when he said he'd call. I gathered I was 'special' enough for the time being.

The following date, another warm evening, found us at a local carnival. It was early June and summer seemed imminent. Pinned up some loose hair and opted to forego outerwear. Light make-up, no bright colors, I wanted Joe to see me as simply feminine and casual. And special, I thought, giggling.

That word puzzled me; connotations of 'special' can be like turning 40, a child with extra challenges, diets that leave out the good stuff—all of those are termed 'special.' Doesn't necessarily mean positive, it means something more to consider. I mulled it over as I waited for him. Rays of sun flooded the living room as the late afternoon wore on and I was covered in hues of pink and gold when he arrived. Again, he was sweating and again, overdressed. I told him that just looking at him made me warm. He took that as a compliment and grinned. My inner self said Buyer Beware while the outer self shrugged and said it's just a date, no big deal.

In the car I noticed small white slivers on the seat of the car and smiled to myself—the guy's eating Mounds candy now! Who could blame him, I had packed in many of those candy bars in my time. Pointing out the coconut to him, he appeared mortified and brushed them away with a fury.

"Joe, it's ok, no big deal," I tried to say. "I like Mounds too-have any more?"

He seemed quizzical for a moment and then relieved as he laughed.

"Hey, Sherlock Holmes," he called me. Whistling now, he tapped to an imaginary beat and I watched the sun disappearing through the window.

At the carnival Joe behaved like a kid, which was endearing. He threw darts at balloons as though his life was on the line, sprayed water seriously into the clown's mouth and looked hungrily at the food stands. He steered me in front of the sausage and peppers booth (how could he know how I loved that?) and bought us big sandwiches and lemonade. A mime, imitating a crying baby in a nearby stroller, caught our attention and we laughed. Joe wiped his forehead off, which was dripping with perspiration, probably due to his noticeable overdressing. The mime spotted him and hugged himself, pretending to be cold, complete with teeth chattering. Joe's face turned red and he sneered at being picked on. His bundling up was more of a problem than he chose to accept.

Back in the car, I noticed more coconut slivers, on the driver's side. I giggled and asked Joe, "Exactly how many of those candies did you sneak in anyway?" Joe seemed still angry as he swept off the residue and slid into the seat. His face was red and stoic. I took a chance and sat a little closer to him, trying to relax the sullen child inside of him. He muttered that I was a pain but a pretty pain at that, and he sighed. He put a Doobie Brothers tape into the deck and we drove home, away from the sights and sounds of the carnival world.

Back home, I insisted he drink a cold soda, and he put his head back on the sofa as I went into my room to change into shorts and a tee. We watched the news and talked about the Yankees. Finally, he removed his jacket and his skin was hot beneath his shirt. I kissed his neck and saw a scaly patch.

"Had a cold," he explained, "and that's what it left. Strange, huh?" Yes, indeedy. I'd had many colds in my life and never was left with one of those. Yet, he was kissing me and that took my focus away. As I wrapped my arms around him, he unbuttoned his shirt, and spoke my name over and over, like Tony sang Maria in West Side Story. With his shirt loosened, I stroked the back of his neck and was aware of skin flaking in my hand. Jerking back, I saw it—skin slivers everywhere! On the couch, on my shorts, on his shoulders, and I involuntarily screamed. It was never Mounds at all—it was Joe.

"No one's perfect, lady. Didn't you ever hear of skin problems? No big deal-don't apologize neither. You're just bursting with compassion, I can see that." His tone dripped with hatred and agony of being found out. I felt revolted and compassion for him, all bunched together.

"Joe, I'm sorry ... but you should have told me. Did you think I'd never notice?" I heard myself swallow the air noisily.

"You know, Tessa, you're no bargain. Your hair is curly and stupid!" And he semi-flew out the door, cursing when he tripped over his size thirteen feet. He banged the outer door and cursed when it refused to open, then seconds later, slammed it as he tore out. I watched our date (and future) end with an uproar.

I vacuumed, took a long, cool shower, sipped an ice water and wondered about all of the strange people out there. Putting my head back on the rocker, I dozed off listening to the late news. I dreamed I was choking on a piece of coconut custard pie.

When I rose the next morning, I poured my coffee and decided that Joe made a huge mistake. That girl who was legally blind? She was the ideal, special woman for him and he let her go. Poor Joe. Poor Coconut Joe.

Roger And The Bellything

With a sterling sense of humor, Roger had me laughing hard during our first telephone conversation. Humor denotes intelligence, and isn't that dreamy, I mused. He joked about his stereotypical Italian grandmother who owned fourteen black dresses, made fun of his numerous allergies (clean air and healthy food) and filled me in on some of the girls he'd dated through the Personal Ads. Always prepared to defend my 'single sisters' my inner self warned me about men who denigrated women. My outer self agreed to meet the comedian at a local diner. He said he'd be wearing a raincoat, his favorite outfit. I hoped he was joking.

After Rudy, my loyal beautician of twelve years had cut off my long hair (into what I insisted upon as "something more chic"), I realized that my hips widened immediately following the hair cut. Armed with a longer jacket, bright lipstick and red nail polish, I planned on keeping Roger's eyes in the right places. I envisioned him as one of those big, warm types of guys who women refer to as "Bear," and who would call me the "little woman." Smiling, we danced to the chapel four weeks later (in my daydream). Be careful, my inner self warned, you're in that sick, romantic mode again. Happens every spring. Take it EASY. The outer self hummed "Love is in the Air" and out the door we all went.

Roger was wearing a greenish-grayish raincoat and as I looked hesitantly, he grinned like a Cheshire cat. He had a round, pudgy face and I noticed a bit of spittle had collected at the corner of his mouth. Nerves, I decided, and tried not to stare at it. We chatted amiably. Roger ordered cheesecake *and* ice cream, (much to my horror) as I opted for one of those oversized cookies. As he gulped his food and I daintily nibbled, he eyed my cookie with adoration. I sensed we'd be sharing it soon.

Roger's choice of topics included a recent allergy, 60's music, and how he memorized the banter between Katherine Hepburn and Spencer Tracy, in all of their movies. Obviously, he didn't date much. Lacking manliness, good manners, or anything worth mentioning, I quickly dismissed that dance to the chapel and concentrated on getting home to some dinner. But then I dropped my napkin and the evening took on a strange twist.

Under the table, groping for the edge of the dancing napkin, I saw what appeared to be a huge package extending from my date's stomach. I softened inside, realizing that he had brought and hidden a gift for me. Maybe he was an artist, and wanted me to see his latest magnificent oil painting.

"Roger, watcha got under the table, huh?" I teased. He looked quizzical. "Whaddya mean?"

"Oh," I said in a singsong voice. "You can show me. I'll pretend I didn't see it, ok?" He dipped my cookie into his soupy ice cream and his expression never changed.

"There's nothing under the table, Tessa, c'mon out from there," he pleaded. He munched another bit of cookie as his shoulders hunched.

"On your lap, silly," I said as I touched it. It was very soft and not a painting or a box of any kind. I fingered it gently. It was a bit lumpy ... it was ... it was ... Roger! It was Roger's enormous body, extending from the gut and my stomach flip-flopped.

"That's not funny, Tessa ... get outa there!" His eyebrows came together and he pouted, with crumbled cookie where the spittle had been. I was mortified for him and felt like I was viewing the freak show at the circus of my youth. It was like a storage compartment, unlike any other stomach I'd seen, including my friend Debbie's, when she had the triplets. I felt so sorry for him.

"Roger, forgive me ... it was a big, no, no, I mean my mistake, not yours ..." I stammered. He looked very sad and stood up. How did I not see that before? His belly dropped below his knees and it was an awesome sight as he looked around the diner self-consciously. Grabbing the last piece of my cookie, he walked away slowly, and never looked back. I took the bill and my wallet and approached the cashier, a lady with exotic looks who now rolled dark eyes and made clucking sounds.

"He likes his desserts, that one," she told me. "He meets ladies here all the time—eats right offa their plates, ya know? He needs to go on a watcha-call, a diet." She raised her mile-long eyebrows at me and I realized she was waiting for a response.

"Yeah," I managed. I nodded as she gave me change and I walked out, still in a haze of that sad young man and his body. Roger was shuffling down the street. No car? Maybe he couldn't fit, maybe he needs drastic surgery. I needed to go home to the sanctity of my little apartment.

Hunger for a meal and weariness were attacking me and the thought of ever eating another big cookie made me queasy. Driving away, I watched Roger in the rear view mirror. He shuffled slowly and became smaller.

He would have liked that. Although I have returned to that diner, I have never seen Roger again. Or ordered an oversized cookie. Good in both cases.

Robert, Not Bob

When I was in high school, I tutored Eddie Milasky in English. His mom paid me but she didn't have to. I was in love with Eddie. He played football and baseball and girls liked him. He was wholesome looking, smelled good, wore red plaid flannel shirts and was comfortable with himself. Eddie was not interested in school subjects unless they were long-legged ones, preferably Gillian Donnelly. She was a cheerleader who had a boyfriend but Eddie just plain made a fool of himself in front of her. On Tuesday's, when I came to his house, and had Eddie to myself, I pretended to be Gillian. I pictured myself blond and athletic and not so smart. Eddie treated me like a teacher, not like a girl his own age. When he got a grade of B, I was proud of us. He gave me a bear hug and I could have easily stayed locked into his arms for the rest of my life. He took two girls to the prom. I was not either of them. When he whirled by me with Adele laughing and enjoying herself, I winked and said, "I can dance better than her, Eddie." And dance I did. Eddie danced a few times with me, and once said he didn't know I was like "this." Well, I was. Tutors can also be girls. We are not robots, I told him, but real girls, just like Gillian Donnelly. He snorted.

"She's an idiot," he said.

"She's the idiot of your dreams, Eddie," I said right back.

"No, you are," he swore, and we both laughed. When he kissed my neck, I would gladly have died then and there.

So when I met Robert, who resembled Eddie, I was light-hearted. "Bob, can I tell you …?"

He cut me right off: "I am not a Bob, always a Robert, if you don't mind, Tessa, ok?"

OK. Eddie had never said he was Edward. Robert sounded stuffy and dull, and I wished for a brief moment that I was far away in an aerobics class. I remembered Eddie and me dancing. I recalled the designer cologne he wore and I breathed in. Go forward, I directed myself. Eddie is from back then and I was here, now. Sometimes we have to go backward, to go forward. Now was that time.

I wrote to Eddie's mother. She said he lived in California, had been writing some screenplays (thanks to me, the tutor) and was vague about his personal life. She didn't quite remember me, either.

"Are you that nice little redhead who tutored him?" she asked, hesitation in her voice.

"No, I'm the brunette who tutored him, from high school," I reminded her.

"Hmmm. I seem to recall you were red-haired. Oh, well," and she kind of closed up.

I waited patiently until that fifteen-year high school reunion. I heard from Roberta Wallace, the big-mouth, professional party planner and reunion organizer (she had been orchestrating events all her life including two divorces) that Eddie was coming in for the reunion.

Words just cannot give adequate vision to the pains I took in readying for this event. Maybe all this Personal Ad stuff could come to a halt, because Eddie would realize I had been his true love all along. I could close my eyes and remember his scent, after football games, of baby talc and spearmint gum. I could feel his hug, even now, and would have to sadly admit that few hugs in the last decade could compare with Eddie Milasky's. I dressed in a fuchsia-colored blouse, with gold sparkly earrings and a quiet gold chain. I wore expensive perfume and brought a tiny beaded purse with me. In it were a small wallet, tissues and spearmint gum. I also had a snapshot of Eddie and me together, working on prom decorations that the music teacher had taken. We looked busy, sloppy and incredibly young.

And there he was. Amidst the low lights and people buzzing around each other, I saw him. He was taller than most, and maintained his good looks. His dirty-blond hair was long and curled up beyond his collar. He looked more casual than was appropriate for the evening but that was forgivable. He was here, and I tried hard not to run toward him but walk, gracefully and like a lady. Inside I was like a young bronco, champing at the bit to be loosed and free.

Eddie smiled lazily and opened those big arms as I ran into them. I heard someone nearby say, "Tessa found her pupil again, would you believe?" I breathed in slowly, taking in Eddie's new scent: tanning lotion, hair gel and a masculinity of some kind. He smelled, well, older.

"Tessa, you are one sweet-lookin' chick. Still a brain?"

"Never was, Eddie. I just always wanted to jump into your pocket, though."

"Dance with me, lady," he demanded. He needn't have. I wasn't going to move away from him no matter what. Not ever.

We danced, slowly and quietly, at first. Then I asked him what he had been up to and my dream machine filled me in.

"I do this and that, Tess. I kind of like no pressure, ya know? No hard drugs, though, just some light refreshments, if you get my drift," he said. I didn't get the drift, didn't want to. He sounded like a wimp, a druggie, a loser. I was horrified. Not Eddie, my Eddie.

"But Eddie ... I heard you were writing, I thought ..." He cut me off.

"That's what Mom thinks. I work, Tess, here and there, don't get me wrong. But no steady stuff. Couldn't handle it. Don't like bosses, don't like routines, ya know? I like the beach, I like freedom, ya know? What about you?" My heart hurt, my throat was very tight.

"I work with abused kids, "I told him. "I think routine is important. Life is rules, Eddie, don't you have some goals, some plans?" I heard myself, horribly whining. But Eddie laughed a gravelly chuckle that reminded me of his young football days.

"Goals, Tess? Yeah. Getting through Mondays to get to Tuesdays. Playing by the rules on the beach. Eating pepperoni pizza on Friday's. Meeting new chicks and old buddies. Speaking of which, excuse me ..." and he sauntered away to say hi to a former teammate, Rich Hilliard. I was stunned. My hands sweated and shook. Eddie was a bum. A good-looking, youthful and funny guy but a bum, who took drugs, didn't work and lazed away on some beach in that land of casual life, California. (My mom's friend had moved there briefly after she became widowed and said "the men here have either two wives or one lung"). I was so devastated. I had built up a scenario of Eddie and me, leaving the reunion, going for coffee, talking about a future together. Now I schmoozed among former old friends and classmates politely, and left the reunion alone, feeling bruised and chilled. The cold air outside felt startling, like a hard slap to the face. When I started my car, I was aware that tears were not too far from brimming and I chided myself.

"Wake up, girl. Fantasy Island is fiction. Real life is this." And then a horrid thought crossed my mind: I would have to continue dating! In the side mirror I saw Eddie, a few football jocks and Gillian Donnelly-Price (now), laughing and looking happy. The old high school feeling of being on the outside of the real—inside-people blanketed me. The tears fell as I drove away from the reunion and into maturity. Good-by Eddie Milasky. Good-by, good-by. It had been a night. I wanted Eddie back, wanted to be in high school again. At home, I would sob and make tea, take out the yearbook and bemoan a few things. Sleep would come and disturbing dreams too. Eddie, if you read this, just know I adored you. I think a part of me still lives in your English book. I relish my old innocence and will always, always love the way we were.

Didn't Barbra Streisand sing that? We all know misery-it grows out of seeds that men drop in our hearts when we're not paying attention.

What the Mom Says

Did I mention that what Mom says almost always mirrors what I feel? We are like that, always have been. She will have a dream about someone and I will bump into them the next day. I will watch a movie and forget an actor's name; she will tell me that name because she needed it that same day doing a crossword puzzle. She is self taught and good at word games. We are alike in that regard. She also likes to hear my dating stories and shakes her head, wondering why her beauty, her talented daughter, her prize, has to endure these creeps. Yes, I concur, why indeed?

Usually we agree in thought.

"So, Tessa, doing anything special this weekend?" she asked recently. I know she wanted me to say breathlessly, "yes, I'm going to accept a marriage proposal from a wealthy doctor, who met you once and adores us both," but no can do. I sigh.

"Like what, Ma?'

"Like go into New York City, see a show, something uplifting. You know." Yes, I do know. Most men won't spring for this kind of date. Dinner is reserved for a second date. Maybe—if there is a second.

"I might go with Jane to a good flea market," I offer.

"Good, that's good. Walking around, picking up odds and ends, maybe, who knows, meet a nice guy ..."

The best part of a flea market is debatable: it may be all the leisurely walking, it may be the endless good buys available, it may be the freedom of being with a longtime girlfriend ... but one thing it isn't? You are not going to meet a nice guy, and better yet, you're not hoping to. No, flea markets are for shoppers and friends wanting to have some time to catch up on one another's lives. A former boyfriend and I used to comb flea markets endlessly but he was the only interesting guy I ever saw at one. No, Jane and I wanted to pick up socks and a few early holiday presents. Period.

"Oh, Ma, not guys again, for pity's sake …"

"Well, I always hope for you. Mothers want to see their daughters settled, you know that. But more, you should have a nice time with Jane, ok, do that."

She's a realist. She knows that time spent with girlfriends is almost always time well spent, with no aggravation and no need to hoard cheesecake at midnight either. Girlfriends are safe.

"Mom, you know what? Let's you and me go to that new movie we talked about, how about it?" Mom, a widow, and I, like to get together. We enjoy each other's company until she brings up THAT topic.

"Ok, honey. We will. And maybe out for a nice supper, my treat."

"It's a date, Mom," I said happily. Dates with Mom were also safe.

Our conversations could range from hours to minutes and are peppered with a few of her wise beliefs. Mom has always lived the golden rule. As a little girl, I believed in it. Now, as a woman, a dating woman, I know better. She speaks excellent English, amusing Yiddish, and is a whiz with grammar. Mom is the person who I feel most comfortable with. When she became widowed at age sixty and went back to working after being a homemaker for forty years, I had great respect for her pluck. Apparently others did also and she became a senior clerk for the county assessor's office. One thing she ruled out however-she would never marry again and she never even dated one man after Dad died.

"Why bother?" she asked, "anyone my age will have his own sicknesses or problems, and who needs it?" Though she may have been fortunate enough to meet a decent guy (and have moved to a large condo in Florida where I could have visited in freezing February), she opted to make a life without the benefit of a gentleman friend. She enjoyed the fun and stress-free socializing with lady—friends, and simply walked away from men as romantic interests. She did not, however, regard that as an option for me. Not even close.

After the movie ("such filthy language," she lamented), we went out for supper, where nearby to our table, a couple quietly argued about money. Then, they ate silently. I felt sorry for the wife.

"See how much more fun we're having?" I said to her.

"Yes, but from me you won't have babies or anniversaries," she answered simply.

Mom calls it as she sees it. So I go on dating, watching for the man who will give me those babies and anniversaries. And give Mom the grandbabies she no doubt dreams about.

Giddyap Mel

Mel Brown had a sort of western twang, which was either authentic (he said he was from Colorado, and how could I know since I'd been in Jersey forever?) or it was practiced. Mel said he liked country/western music and began a litany of songs and performers, of whom I only recognized one: Loretta Lynn and that was because I'd seen Coal Miner's Daughter every time it was on TV.

Mel said he was a natural cowboy and would like to meet me at the ONE country bar in our urban county, then named the Heartland Café. I agreed, mainly out of curiosity.

When I arrived at the place and could hear country music blaring (the songs all sounded strangely alike to my ears), I hoped the man outside waving wasn't waving to me. He was. Mel looked like (and proudly) an Elvis wannabe. His blue leisure suit with sequins was sparkling in the moonlight and his long sideburns, buffalo-shaped belt buckle and toothpick emerging as he greeted me made me want to pretend I was someone else. Kind of like *he* was doing. He shook my hand mightily and called me 'gal' and I felt the headache coming on before we entered the smoke-filled, crowded place. What I saw in there amazed me. Women with full skirts, some with poodles on them, others with musical notes (all so vintage) danced in lines with men gawking. Some chewed bubble-gum, some wore bright pink lipstick and several had on little boots. Many were decked in pretty but see-through blouses. Several wore stacked and numerous bracelets, rings and earrings in Native American style, and one even had long dark braids down her back. The dancing seemed rhythmic and foreign. The band played sulky, loud music and Mel grabbed my hand. Even some of the 'regulars' (I imagined they were) kind of laughed at his appearance. Or maybe they were laughing at me, and rightfully so.

Mel said something to me and his breath was terrible-oniony and sour, and I swallowed, and then averted my head. His flat oily hair was cut all uneven, and we knew then Mel had taken hold of those kitchen scissors, probably just before he left his house. A cowboy hat on a table had buttons all over it including one that read: "No fat chicks." I was sickened and didn't belong here, any more than I belonged at a Klan rally.

I prayed that no one here would know me and that I could escape really soon without Mel making a big noise about it or worse—following me. He would be the type, to see that the 'little lady' got to her car safely.

Mel's dancing was killing him; huge sweat spots were lining his shirt and as he turned around and grinned like a fool, I thought of Clint Eastwood shooting Mel, out of respect for decent people everywhere.

At some point, Mel admitted that he'd only visited Colorado, but had loved it so much there, he 'adopted' it as his birthplace. The truth was he came from West Cooneystown, a blue collar town in upstate New York. So not "western." I had had relatives from there, and remembered dingy apartments close to one another, mainly filled with immigrants and smoky rooms. Now, it had been built up, with upscale condominiums and restaurants. Mel didn't belong there either.

"Why did you lie, Mel?" I asked.

"Well, I um, wanted to um, impress you. Stupid, huh?" I hoped that was rhetorical.

I thought about this. Mel could not have impressed anyone, anywhere, about anything.

"Mel, you know what? You need some mints … and you need to be honest," I said, and didn't add that he also needed—desperately—a shower and a day with an image consultant.

He laughed, saying something about lovin' those fried onions, and he blew out a host of bad air right into my face. This cracked him up and he grabbed my hand to dance again. He stepped, rotated his hips, dosie-doed and smiled happily at himself in the big mirror overhead. I smiled back, then moved back, back, back, until I was in the doorway while he was still enamored with himself on the dance floor.

I smiled at the bouncer (a big blond with a white cowboy hat-the good guy, right?) and stepped out into the cool night air, taking deep breaths. A couple of girls were walking in, with skin-tight bell-bottom jeans, high, high heels and teased up hair. I looked at my watch. It was early enough to stop and get a pizza to bring home with a rented movie. I wanted now more than ever to get back into the decade I had left for a few hours. I saw a couple dancing through the window, and doggone if it wasn't Mel with a pretty blond. She was wearing a tee shirt, decorated by thousands of little silver guitars. They were a perfect couple. I almost skipped to my car and watched Mel wink at Blondie. They were sharing urban love.

Happy Trails, you two. And I hotfooted my pony outa there. It had been a time.

That Former Boyfriend, Again

I s it just me? Running into "exes" when least expected? Rory (real name Robert but he liked Rory better-that should have ended it then and there) appeared during a recent bagel stop. He stood on line, baseball cap slightly ajar, and looking boyish. Rory was not a considerate boyfriend but we had gone together years ago for a year or so, until we both tired of trying to remake each other over. He needed some consciousness training and I needed my head examined for dating him. He had a bunch of habits (sniffling, pointing when speaking to you, standing too close and chewing/blowing bubble gum, to name a few beauties) and they eventually got to me. That, and also that he was dating a younger, skinnier girl than me, at the same time. Her name was Tiffany and I knew I would not like her.

Now, however, he looked wonderful. Cute, animated, fresh-faced. He wore a tee-shirt bearing the name of some team in a southern state and cutoff jeans shorts. He sniffled, then noticed me and uneasily said, "Well, hi." I smiled, nodded and felt too warm. An old lady in line grinned at me. "Go for it," she whispered too loudly. I rolled my eyes and wondered again, is it just me?

He ordered twenty-four bagels and the line moved. As he turned to leave, he stopped briefly to say, "I learned a lot these past coupla years. From you, just life, ya know? And let's talk, how about it?"

I assumed he meant by phone, so I gave him my number, the old lady hummed happily and soon I got my bagel, my lone bagel, and wondered why Rory ordered twenty-four.

Rory and I were very casual in our early relationship, more like two old friends. Not too many sparks flew as his social habits wore on me. Yet he was very polite, his mother was a sensational cook and I spent joyful times at his house, watching videos and playing cards with the family. His dad was quiet and didn't have a personality that I could see. His mom and I were more like sisters and the dog, a poodle, was hyper like Rory. Rory's mind raced. He didn't relax well and my family saw him as hard working, serious. To me, he was hung up on not feeling useful if he wasn't working on something. He wasn't romantic and didn't seem to think he needed that. He was an original 'chick magnet', though, because he was so completely … well, male. I had missed him. Or missed having a boyfriend who demanded little.

And now, we talked. The ducks in this park were outnumbering the foolish humans who fed them. Like me. They quacked and we spoke.

"Tiffany left me for a married guy, wouldja believe that?"

Was he asking? Of course she had. Tiffany was fake, Tiffany was for a season. Men don't get it.

"Married guys can't commit," I explained. The rules of dating, 101.

"Some women, that's enough for them." I finished.

He looked pained. He had loved her.

"How come you were buying twenty-four bagels?" I blurted.

"Oh, for work, my staff," he said offhandedly. *My* staff? He was a big cheese? Hard to imagine.

"I have a marketing company, Tessa. We advertise, sell lists, right up there in Fort Lee, ya know? Right across from your beloved New York."

He and I had wandered aimlessly around New York City. It had been his beloved New York too. I always loved that place until a friend was assaulted in her apartment. I had slept over there only a week earlier. It changed me, the way the movie Jaws stopped me from going out real far into the ocean.

Rory and I had walked, arm in arm, all over New York. We were kids, hung up on each other's looks and simple youth. I studied him now and could feel the same way.

"Tessa, I cheated on you. I have to come clean about that. I really loved Tiff, ya know? She cheated on me, it's a cycle. If it makes ya feel better, I go for therapy."

Therapy over getting dumped? I'd never be *out* of therapy if I sought a counselor every time a male said "I'll call you" and didn't. How did Rory get that weak?

"Yeah, I'm learning to build up my inner resources," he said happily.

Sighing, I put my arm around him. I kissed him on the cheek before I stood up and gave him the loaf of bread.

"Rory, you'll make it, really you will. Glad I saw you. Have a good life, buddy," I called as I left. He nodded and fed the eighteen noisy ducks that had found their new best friend.

It is true-you can never go home again. And if you do, don't go back to the boyfriend you left there. The reason you left? You'd leave again, same same.

Meow Man

Larry and I met at a little pub in nearby Lincoln City. They made great hamburgers there, Larry had said, and since I'd been a burger fan for bunches of years, this was an ideal date already.

He had on an oversized tee shirt with a huge longhaired cat emblazoned on the front. I thought that was real strange for a guy but it wasn't offensive or gross. "Hey," he said and that was all he said. He half-smiled and his jittery nerves were showing.

"Hiya, Larry, how are you?" I greeted him. He sucked on his top lip, nodded his head instead of saying he was fine and I believed then he should have had "wimp" imprinted on his forehead at birth.

Larry was a bookkeeper and didn't deal with people much in his job, and admitted to shyness. I asked him about his shirt and he brightened.

"That's Drucilla, my cat. Isn't she the most?" The most 'what' I wasn't sure about, but she was the largest thing I'd ever seen on a shirt before.

"She looks real pretty," I offered. And that began a discussion on Drucilla. Her looks, habits, behavior, history and much, much more. I was so bored and Larry was so excited.

"And she comes when I call her and she can dance, and sing? You should hear her meow when I put the radio on—country, of course, she really likes Tanya Tucker—and she's...."

"But Larry, tell me about YOU," I interrupted. His face fell. His spark just went right out. He picked up his (now surely cold) burger.

"Not much to say," he said and munched sadly.

"Well, what do you like to do outside the house?" I tried.

"Well, I like to take pictures. And ride my bike. Sometimes, I take Dru with me, well, she rides in a little basket in the front. You should see her, so cute up there...." And so it went.

As the Christmas holidays were approaching, I asked him about his plans. I was desperate to end this feline evening. I didn't mention my cat allergies.

"Well, I'll probably visit the folks in Michigan," he said, "but Dru hates the long travel, and I never know what to buy anyone anymore. But I bought Dru five gifts already...."

I couldn't bear it, not one more minute. I told Larry I needed to get home and he took the check generously. He also gave me a brotherly hug and wished me well. I told him to have a wonderful Christmas and that maybe the New Year would bring the "right" girl into his life (because it sure wasn't me). He shrugged.

"I'm tired of lookin, ya know? I think maybe Dru and I might be it. What do you think?" I wouldn't dare tell him what I thought.

"Well, never give up. Maybe when you're not looking ... you know. Take it one day at a time, ya know?" I didn't know what to say. He needed counseling, several sessions at least. He said goodbye, waving at me and the last thing I remember is that when his arm went up, so did the cat's tail on his shirt.

I pulled out of the parking spot, joined the traffic. I pictured Larry going home too, with "Dru" running to meet him and asking him,

"So, how was it? Was she better than me?" The cat asked.

Truly I was losing my mind. At home, I changed into sweats, made tea and called my friend Dana.

"Hi. Guess what? I'm home already. What a night! I met a guy who is in love with his cat," I told her. There was silence, then a kind of chuckle.

"Was he named Larry?" she asked. I sighed. And we laughed as only girl friends can.

Holiday Guy

Nick McCabe was already interesting during our first conversation. "Tessa, that's a cool name. Are you cool?" I thought so, definitely cool. The name Nick McCabe was unusual, I thought, and said so.

"Well, mom's Greek, her name's Athena, would you believe, and my Dad was a rip-roarin' Irish drunk. Gone now, drank himself into oblivion. Anything else you need to know?"

I hadn't even needed to know all that, I thought. The devilish spirit on my right shoulder thought he was original and whispered "go for it," while the guardian angel on the left told me this one was way too weird to believe. Back and forth, I vacillated, but as usual, I had to take the dare. I was pleasantly surprised—at first.

Nick and I looked well together. He was a big guy, broad shouldered and rugged. He limped. He said he was once in a motorcycle accident. I didn't want/ask for details because it wasn't my need to know. He said he loved my long crazy curls and I remembered to toss them every few minutes.

We went "malling" which is a great first date. We people-watched, drank coffee, ate cookies and laughed. But when Nick talked about his Mom, (and he even said Mom in two syllables, so slowly) he made me think she might be more spiritual than earthly. He raved about her cooking, her tone of voice, her smart decisions. (Not too smart staying married to a "rip-roarin' drunk", I thought). He put her on a pedestal. That was not only a red flag, but it was waving. Despite that, we had fun and decided to get together the following week. The Christmas holidays were approaching and I think we both wanted dates for New Year's (that night that can be dreadful to those single-wannabe-married types).

Twice more we dated, and during our second, an afternoon, we went Christmas shopping together at the mall. How can you not be cheerful at the mall during the holidays? The intercom music was playing carols, kiosks were buzzing with business, Christmas decorations were magnificent—it was delightful. Nick McCabe said he wanted to get his Mom something special, something that he does each year. I knew he wanted me to guess what he was planning and so I asked, "A fur jacket?" It was something I wanted, so why not get him thinking, haha? He shook his head no and I noticed, for the first time, that one ear was smaller than the other. The motorcycle accident?

No, he had something really special in mind. Actually, he said he does it every year, and she waits for this gift. A day trip to a spa? A bus trip? Gift certificates? No, no and no, he said. I gave up. I should have.

No, Nick McCabe, the Greek-Irishman said, he waits until the mall quiets down and then he sits on Santa's lap for a picture. I burst out laughing, and waited for him to join me. Didn't happen.

"Nick," I kept choking, "aren't you a little old and big for that? I asked and answered. He bit his lip.

"It's what she wants," he said with no shame. I watched him go up to Santa when there was no line, and I noticed that the poor fellow in the red suit shuddered a bit just before Nick climbed up.

Remember I asked how anyone could not feel cheerful at the mall during the holiday season? Well, I found a way. I was mortified when a senior couple walked by and stopped abruptly, not believing their eyes. I acted bored and disinterested lest they think I was attached in any way to this fool.

And so, Nick McCabe and I went our separate ways, immediately following his photo shoot (he dropped me off without asking why I was mute the entire ride home). I spent New Year's with my sister and a few other dateless folks who ate Chinese food and made merry. I could not bear dating a man who would climb atop Santa Claus for his mother or any other reason. Sigh. I should have made a resolution to stop dating then and there. But you know how "they" say the man of your dreams can be right around the corner? I had to hope for that and keep on walking.

Bridge People

Tony sounded like an enchanting, whimsical kind of person. He told me he was an investment banker, played harmonica, idolized Jerry Lewis (and we'd both done telethon volunteer work for years) and liked to explore nature when he hiked. He was against all substance uses—said his brother died an alcoholic. He did not ask me what I looked like, what my sign was or anything too, too personal. He had a warm voice, coated with throaty interest and an occasional manly chuckle. Wonder why he hadn't been married yet, I thought.

It would not be long before I would get an answer to this.

He said walking, long walks across bridges, along creeks and through woods relaxed him. I agreed heartily to meet him one Saturday morning, on the New Jersey side of the George Washington Bridge, where we'd walk across and back, enjoying the view of New York City.

And so we met. Tony was not handsome and not homely either. I guess he was an average looking fellow. We both wore blue jeans and red shirts, and laughed at our twin outfits. He had on high-top sneakers and I wore old, comfy Keds. We walked and talked. He brought granola treats for both of us; I had brought popcorn. I guess we figured that just by looking at the Hudson River, we wouldn't be thirsty.

Tony had been exceptionally close to the brother who died, but he had figured out a way to "bring him back." I know people who communicate with the departed and I had never much respected or believed in that. But it fascinated me anyway.

"Yeah, I can actually bring him to me," said Tony, whose face now glowed.

"Can others see him when you do?"

"If they want to, sure," he offered.

I didn't want to so that left me out. But I wondered how he thought he did this. So I asked.

"Well, it happens mainly on hikes. Like now. I can get Phil to visit, walk along with me. He once brought a buddy who had died two years before him, in a car crash. That was amazing," he finished.

Amazing is a good word. It also describes the kind of single men out there that we ladies have to experience. It is amazing that there are so many weirdos. Maybe he would be angry that I didn't believe him and want to give me a shove. Right off the bridge, down, down I would go. I was scaring myself.

"Let's talk about something else," I said uneasily.

"Creeping you out?" Tony said without making eye contact.

"Yes. And we're almost at the halfway point, between New York and New Jersey. I like to take note of being in two states at the same time."

"Uh-huh," he said quietly. And Tony suddenly stopped still, closing his eyes. Then they popped open.

"Great news!" he screamed. "Phil is coming right now!"

I watched a couple stroll by, hand in hand, on the other side of the bridge. Why was it so hard to just find someone normal, someone who would take my hand and lead the way to an average life, a home, a couple of kids, the proverbial dog … I sighed. Phil, the dead brother was on his way.

"Tell him you have company and you'll catch up with him later," I begged.

"He has left upper heaven already. I can feel his presence …" and Tony rocked a little on the heels of his high tops. A passing woman stared at him.

"Is he all right?" she asked, concerned.

"Not really," I said, "he's just waiting for his dead brother to come down now and meet me. From upper heaven."

The woman scowled and left us in a hurry. I poked Tony lightly on the forearm.

"Hey, buddy, you ok?" He still hadn't opened his eyes. I looked around. A beautiful sailboat went by underneath us with the magnificent view of majestic New York City in sharp focus. I worried about this investment broker who was certifiably nuts and was now rocking, eyes closed, on this bridge. I hoped this was all a joke on me but I doubted it. Tony opened his eyes and looked at me, pointedly.

"He went back up," he seethed "he sensed your disbelief. I can't believe you, Tessa."

I couldn't believe my dumb luck either. I had to meet this man who wasn't content to be with just me but had to have his brother along to chaperone. A dead brother yet. What on earth was I doing here? I inhaled. Hard.

"Tony, I am sorry but I just don't think it's healthy, what you're doing. However, it's your brother and your life. I'm moving on," and indeed I did. I bolted, and popcorn bounced into the mighty Hudson as I left this newest collection of crazies behind. I jogged without looking back. His mouth open, he called me and started to run too, but he didn't catch up. At the bus station on the New York side, I jumped onto the first bus going back to New Jersey and stared out the grimy window. I called out to God: "Please, if you're listening, please stop me from dating these nut-jobs. Thank you. Oh, and say hi to Phil if you have him there," I added.

Now TV shows are ripe with people who communicate with the dead, there are books about channeling, visions, all of it. I know it isn't in keeping with my own beliefs and I think it's a big scam. But Tony has used it to not accept his brother's death. I could not date someone who is this stuck and sick, and seeking unhealthy means as therapy. I would rather be alone forever.

And judging by my track record, it seemed it might just go that way.

The "X" in Ex-Husband

At any given time, we can expect to run into the ex-husband (exes?). Hopefully it is not when we look raggedy, tired or unhappy. It is best to have these encounters when we are arm-in-arm with a handsome date or laughing heartily with our girlfriends. Of course, neither of those tends to happen. At the market gazing at cupcakes (but really needing broccoli), I ran into Seth.

"Hey, Mrs. Berger, the first, how are ya?" and I grimaced. Seth had married quickly after our divorce, then once again years later. He was presently in a living arrangement with a woman who raised monkeys, I was told. To me, that fit.

"Well, hello back to ya," I sounded fake even to myself.

"Still like that cake, huh? I remember ... remember what I liked?" And how I did. He ate mini-donuts non-stop. And took insulin and cholesterol medicine, both. However, now he was trim, gray and shorter, and seemed sort of judgmental as his eyebrows raised at me. I felt chubby and ashamed. Why couldn't we have met at the produce section?

"Yeah, you like donuts, right?" I smiled.

"Not anymore, no, that's gone, gone with the wind ... gone with the wives!" He laughed. "No, now it's granola, Centrum, good stuff. I feel better too," he said.

I nodded. He looked healthier and maybe less jumpy, but now he seemed self-righteous.

"Well, what have you been up to? Have kids yet?" He knew my hot buttons. I shook my head, as I heard the biological clock make loud ticking sounds inside my heart. I wondered if I would ever have the children I so wanted, the ones he had with wife Number Two.

"Well, Ricky's nine now and Kimmie is six, and I'm having a new one, in a couple of months. Who would have thought?" I tried to smile but my mouth wouldn't do it.

When Seth and I married many moons ago, I would have thought it. He was the type who would be a good dad, I had believed. If he hadn't been addicted to pain killers and had personality changes too intense for me, we would have had that Ricky and Kimmie ourselves, and maybe even a third one. I sighed.

"Sorry, Tessa, didn't mean to make you feel bad. But you have loads of time, girl. You'll be a great mommie. My partner raises monkeys, would you believe, and the kids love them-they sleep with 'em. Sometimes we all sleep together, it's a blast. Well, gotta run, but you look good, girl, really you do. Take care, get married already, have them kids," and he was off. White noise raged in my head from him, as it did all those years ago. His voice, his thinking. I had forgotten how I was so relieved when he moved out, back to his parent's house and out of ours.

And they all slept together? Like a zoo, I thought. Gross. Yet, it sounded like fun and how life was supposed to be, silly, loving, and noisy. I turned away from the cupcakes, away from the thinking of What Might Have Been. It's second to If Only, and I had vowed not to go there, not to feel that anymore.

I gathered up a few groceries and tried not to jealously watch Seth climb into his minivan as I checked out. He was more agile and purpose-ful. He and I had visited flea markets, museums, and parks, always full of talk, always eating junk food, and he always needed pills for a back that gave him chronic pain. He was not my parents' dream of a husband, but they accepted him. My dad didn't like his unembarrassed way of display-ing affection for me in front of anyone, and his open admission to "eat-ing" pills for dessert. Yet, when he left me, my dad was warm and admit-ted that Seth was "darn likeable" and didn't dwell on all the bad things I was rid of. For that, I was and remain, very grateful.

So, you have to get past that encounter, ride it out. It's okay if you cry in the car or grit your teeth or hurt for a while. I chose to get on the bike and pedal with a vengeance, followed by a trip to the pizzeria.

Cheaper than therapy and did the trick. That night, I watched reruns of The Odd Couple and thought of Seth, his "partner", kids and monkeys, and decided that was entirely too odd for me. I slept well. It was night and then day, just like the Good Book promises. There is comfort in the way time moves along, ordering us to begin anew. And so I did.

Conrad From Someplace Else

He was a scary looking man with dark eyes, a pale scar over his lip and a meanness that caused me to shiver. Why don't we pay attention to our inner voices? "He looks scary but maybe it's nerves," I said to myself, excusing him from being a psychopath.

We met at a lake I like to go to where Canada geese aren't shy about wanting to be fed. We walked around tossing bread out to the noisy, flapping birds and getting to know one another.

Conrad admitted he was 'old-fashioned' and didn't go for trendy people, places or things. He liked traditional marriage (yes, I wanted to scream, I believe in that too!), no alternate lifestyles, wholesome movies.

We talked about movies but he didn't seem to know any recent titles. He was unfamiliar with books I read and never had heard of Liza Minelli. That did it for me.

"Are you serious? Cabaret? New York, New York? She's Judy Garland's daughter, c'mon, you must know her."

Conrad shook his head. Another faint scar on his cheek went out toward his ear, and it was menacing. He liked John Wayne, Ursula Andress and a few now-deceased stars from eons ago. He was creepy. He was not for me.

"Does anyone call you Connie?" I asked.

"They better not," he growled, and put a firm arm around my waist. "Walk this way," he commanded. We were walking away from the parking lot, toward an unfamiliar street.

"No, Conrad, back this way," I turned sharply. His grip tightened.

"If you don't let go, I'll scream, and I'm LOUD," I said that in my best director voice. He grinned and to my relief, took his arm away.

"Didn't mean to scare ya, I have a controlling nature, sorry about that. Ladies need men's protection, ya know?"

I nodded and walked to my car. Conrad looked sad.

"I shoulda tole ya. I was locked up for armed robbery, fifteen years. I got out last year, been datin', turned my life around. It's ain't easy, Tess, ya know? Like I try, ok? But I have my moments, bad dreams. But I'm comin' together, yer a social worker, ya should understand me, right?"

Right. I understand. I understand that I want to be far away from criminals, even ones that have done their time. I cannot relate to their dreams, their choices, and their lives gone badly. It's one thing professionally, another personally for my future.

"It's not that Conrad," I said quietly, "I couldn't go with a guy who doesn't just love Liza Minelli. She's great. And it's getting late, and I have to go, sorry." I gunned the engine, fear prickling me all over.

The next day I changed my telephone number and found myself watching the rearview mirror for a couple of weeks. I never saw Conrad again but I'll bet he has a tight grip on some poor girl out there somewhere, who doesn't care about that scar or that Conrad served time. She isn't a Liza fan either, no doubt.

That night, I showered twice and watched a rerun of M.A.S.H. I laughed and got Conrad out of my system. I had a dream about loud voices and geese behind bars. Conrad lurked in my subconscious for a short time. So many misfits, so few good dates. I closed my eyes and tried to remember the last good time I had as a teenager. It was in eighth grade, with a love interest named Stuart. He made me a grilled cheese sandwich and stroked my face. I believed I would always be the kind of girl men went nuts on. Stuart was very handsome and friendly, and chose me, for a while, to be the girl who rode on his bike and who shared ice cream with him. He called me Tessa-girl and I whirled inside to a song that no one else could hear. Stuart gave me hope for being a popular, sought-after type. He carved our initials into the family oak tree. He loved me.

Sadly, it didn't exactly work out. He died in a freak accident and now I can't call him to save me from this endless array of dates. But I call him in my dreams and I speak to him when I'm alone. I believe he kind of set me up and is responsible for all these dates I have to endure. He should have not been drinking beer and driving, and we could have been married now. Conrad would have been a stranger, not a man who entered (and exited) my life. Stuart made me believe that I would always attract men easily, like a remote control.

He was so wrong. But I go on, trying.

Deathly Conversations

There were a few men whose conversations were so awful or unhealthy that dates (wisely on my part) never materialized. Some were not even worth telling you because they were dull or lacked imagination or weren't memorable. Still, there were these, because they made me laugh, made me sick or made me think. You may even know some of these people and if so, I hope you dismissed them as easily as I did.

Vern, the Slender

Vern and I had missed about three calls from each other (so said the answering machine; how did we ever live without them?) and by the time we spoke, I was already enthused. Human nature makes us thrill to what we do not know. Vern had described himself in his ad as "kind of average, blue eyes (both), like to read, do puzzles, visit zoos and take photographs." He sounded almost too wholesome, a little like me. And a lot like my elderly Aunt Lottie from Atlantic City, who liked the beach and occasionally skipped along the shoreline to music playing only in her mind.

We spoke for a while discussing pet ownership, morning talk shows (was he home ill too, I hoped, as opposed to unemployed?) and the eternally troubled Middle East. Then, the bombshell: "And by the way, I'm slender, are you?" In all my born days, I never heard a man say he was slender. Not a heterosexual one. I could never be described in that way nor did I wish to date someone who found that necessary to ask. "No, Vern," I told him truthfully, "I'm a big girl—tall and wide-hipped, pleasingly plump." Not pleasing to him, I'll bet, judging by the silence on the other end. His voice found itself: "Oh, then, there's a problem, you see." (He heaved a loud sigh here, indicating a profound thought would follow) "I can't get turned on unless a chick is slender, like me." He honestly said 'chick.' Was I supposed to respond, I wondered? I shuddered. I looked up heavenward and shrugged off the gross sensations I was having. Why was I forced to endure this? "Well," I said, "Vern, I just gotta go. Hope you meet the skinniest lady of your dreams, jogging and starving herself—good luck, really, you will need it." I burst out laughing seconds before I heard him click off. Sigh.

Jake, Loving Jake

Jake was a bartender, but once, he said in almost a whisper, he played in the minor leagues. Baseball, he said. When I didn't say, "Oh, wow!" I think he felt rejected. Once I tried out for a local movie role too but it doesn't make me Meg Ryan now, does it?

"I like to dance, I like people, what do you like?" he asked breathlessly.

"I like giraffes," I told him.

"Huh, giraffes? Yeah, ok, I like them. I'm tall too. But mostly I like tigers, so beautiful, so sleek, I'm kind of like that …"

I shuddered. He was so in love already with him, there was no extra space, no room in there for me. Let alone my giraffe …

"Jake, I'm a social worker, what do you do?"

"I do it all, Tess, can I call you that? I sing, dance, counsel the lonely, hey, and I look like Tom Cruise in Cocktail, didja see that?"

Yeah, and I'm Miss America. Did you ever wish you could slap someone's face? I, the pacifist, who can still cry at any act of violence, wanted to hurt, really smash Jake.

"Jake, you tend bar, right? Do you go to school?"

"Not right now, no time for that … I keep long hours. But don't worry, I've got intelligence, I'm real smart, like, everyone comes to me with their personal life, and I, like solve their problems." I am sure he does as he refills their whiskey glasses and hears the ka-chink of business a-growin' all night long.

"Jake, I think I'm going to excuse myself now, I'm late for exercise class. Good luck with your life, although you probably don't need it," I said.

"Hey, Tessa, now wait up! I'm willin' if you are, I mean, c'mon, let's meet and see it through, this date thing. I like babes who exercise." He sounded desperate and like he enjoyed hearing his own voice.

"Bye, Jake, let's not, and you take care …" And I hung up. He did call once after that but after a second refusal, his pride said to knock it off. I wanted to thank that vanity from the depths of my heart.

Weirdo

Merle had answered my ad; he had an adolescent voice and I winced as it went up and down the scale, like a badly tuned trombone. He was a sales associate for a 'major retailer' he wouldn't name. Sure.

"Why can't you say where you work, Mel?"

"It's Merle. And because you might go there and check me out prior to the date. That would be unfair, right Tessy?"

"It's Tessa. And yeah, that would be an unfair advantage, sure would. Hmm."

He breathed a sigh of relief into my ear and chatted easily about liking rare steak, parmy potatoes (give me a break) and baking goodies with his dad, only he had never met his dad, so he baked and pretended they were in the kitchen together. He liked making cookies with little faces on them; his father would tell him what expressions to make. I closed my eyes and prayed for the umpteenth time to deliver me from this, please Lord.

"Excuse me, Mel, but …"

"It's MERLE!"

"Merle, forgive me for interrupting but we're not compatible. And I'm late for something."

I hung up rather sharply and went right into the freezer. Scooping out the ice cream, I wondered how I would have the strength to date again. I smoothed chocolate marshmallow all over my tongue and basked in the glory of being alone in my tiny kitchen with this dessert. Should I put Cool Whip on it or not? Maybe I should ask Mel's, no Merle's, father.

Ian the Scholar

Ian and I hit it off on our first conversation, but he was just leaving for an appointment and had to phone me back a few nights later. He liked to discuss the world's issues, morals, ethics, "real stuff," as he said. After twenty minutes of real stuff, I wanted to know trivia: what do you like to do, have you traveled, who's in your family, the kind of stuff that makes you real. He was reluctant.

"Well, let's save that for another time, ok? But have you heard that we've spent over $40 billion on AIDS and less than half on mental health counseling of our juveniles? Seems to me …"

"Ian, I need to hear the 'real' stuff at this point. We may agree on ethics but if you hate your mother, we're nowhere, ok?"

"I don't hate her," he said thoughtfully. "But she's not my favorite person. Enough about me, tell me about you," he said. Seriously.

"I love my mother, "I told him. "I have great friends, a challenging career, and am usually very upbeat. Are you?"

"Why do you ask?" he said and I just knew any date with him would be far too long. We hung up shortly after that and I never regretted it.

These are a sampling. Now come along on a few more actual dates. Come, bring a friend and a barf bag. You will need both.

Tommy, Once a Cop

You know this type: tall, strong looking, a tad too much gut, nose slightly red … dark eyes, furtive, chewing gum, smells wonderful of musky cologne. This type calls waitresses "hon" and those gals smile big toothy grins at these guys. They look ready to pounce but control their movements like well-rehearsed actors. Their clothes are immaculate, smartly pressed, and their shoes shine like mirrors. Their hair is slicked back and wouldn't dare misbehave. These are former policemen or detectives who are now security guards or private investigators. They are semi burned out, middle-aged and hot to trot. They have great stories to tell. They expect women to give of themselves and they usually aren't disappointed.

Their marriages took a beating and their kids adore them. They have no memories of family outings but can recall every day on the squad with poignancy. These men make for very nice occasional dates but never, ever expect them to commit—even to the next date. They will take you out to their favorite eateries or clubs and expect some old-fashioned loving in return. If you refuse, you will never see them again. For that, you are most fortunate.

I met a unique one. We never quite made it through that first date even. Tommy met all of the above qualifications. Years of observation and dating taught me how to dress that evening: a feminine white blouse, cranberry slacks, tiny pearl earrings, you get the picture. My image screamed conservative, I-know-how-you-good-ole-boys-like-us. Tommy smiled, exposing little white pearly teeth (definitely not the originals) and a slight dimple. Cute for an older guy.

"Hey, Miss Tess, nice to meetcha," he said gallantly. The slight frown on his face I couldn't read. Yet.

The hotel where we met was lovely; the top floor lit up with tiny blinking lights along the molding and a view of New York City in the background. Carnations adorned the vases that elegantly sat on crisp, white linen tablecloths. I smiled my best first-date smile and knew exactly what to say:

"It's nice to meet you, Tommy. Tell me about yourself." And they love that because they are comfortable with this subject. I would interrupt only once or twice, to laugh or share a story too, but mostly I would let him talk. I thought it might be very nice to slow dance with this man.

Tommy ordered our drinks ("hiya, hon, the lady will have …") and I observed his cuff links initialed TTC (Tommy, The Cop?). He made polite chatter and caught the eye of an old buddy across the room. They raised chins at one another and seemed to say, "Catch ya later," without actually saying a word. We clinked our glasses together (his scotch and my diet Pepsi) and they made a pretty sound. He talked some more about his police work, and again, he made a face I couldn't quite get a handle on. His brow came together and then, he noisily snapped his fingers.

"Aha!" he said with triumph.

"Aha?" I repeated.

"Tess, you won't believe this, but you look like my ex! I couldn't figger it out at first, why I instantly felt weird around you. That's it! You look like her, well I'll be darned," he said happily.

"Felt weird?" I sounded like a parrot.

"Yeah, and I thought, gee, was I nervous … or what? But I knew it wasn't me. It was you! Wow, I feel better." And the jerk was grinning.

"So … how much do I look like her?" I gathered the slow dance was out of the picture for sure.

"Too much," he kept grinning. "I mean, we can sit here, but I ain't marrying ya or nuthin. It's amazing that two women can look alike, that much. Wait, maybe I have an old picture," and he proceeded to pull out his wallet. I stood up.

"Where ya goin?" He seemed surprised that I was unenthused.

"I think I need some fresh air. And your buddy wants to talk to you, so let me say good night right here. It's been … interesting," I noticed his wallet open, to a blond woman's picture. Seemed he kept all of the ex's pictures maybe.

"Hey, don't be like that, I don't mind, you can't help it," he whined. I never looked back and got on the elevator in a flash. Joining me was an older woman, smiling, knowing. I bit my lip.

"Men, right? Unbelievable. Here you are, all prettied up … running for your life." And she told me her latest battle scar on the way down.

"Hey, between the Internet, my therapy and the two cats, who has time for this crap anymore?" and she smiled, showing me bright pink lipstick smeared on both front teeth. I shrugged and shook my head.

The fresh air was wonderful. I walked to my car and wondered why Tommy, middle-aged and experienced in life, was clueless about the nuances of first dates. "I wouldn't marry ya or nuthin," he had said. I looked up into the night heavens and silently thanked God for that. And so much more.

Tommy, you none-too-bright fool, you need to practice first dates, learn some manners and never, ever darken my doorstep. I found my car, unobtrusive and waiting for me. Safely seated and with the car started, I heard myself let out a long sigh. I must be getting tired of this dating routine. Maybe it was time to quit for a few months. This was Wednesday.

"Can't quit. I have a date Saturday. Mike something. Onward and upward," I said to the passing cars. I went home and ate a BIG piece of cheesecake. Unfortunately, that was the highlight of the evening.

Mike, the Schnozz

Mike Lewis had the most bulbous, enormous nose I had ever seen. On this mild Saturday evening, with a hint of spring in the air and a perfect 'date' night, here I was, staring (trying not to be obvious) up into a hideous sight. It was wide, hooked and each nostril looked large enough to consume an entire tissue.

I only hoped I didn't blurt out anything mean. It was like tiptoeing around an elephant. His car was very neat and clean, although he had "Let's Go Mets" decals on the glove compartment, which seemed childish. He was tall, very tall, at least 6'3" with a shock of reddish hair (receding of course, only criminals like John Gotti have great hair after middle age) and some freckles. He was too old to be cute and his nose was too big to ignore. His hands, when he shook mine, were clammy and nail-bitten. Another short evening, I could see.

"Didja see the game Saturday?" he asked.

"The truth?" I asked and he nodded, like a sixth grader.

"I'm a Yankees fan," I admitted. He whistled.

"Whoa, I never dated a Yankee fan. This is neat-o. Want to go to a game sometime, I mean a Mets game," he said.

"Never," I told him. He laughed and scratched that big nose. I gritted my teeth.

He shared that he loved hamburgers, hot dogs and flea markets, in that order. I shared that I liked hamburgers, reading and manicures, and added the ocean, to outdo him.

"Yeah, them waves," he said. "Let's go to the beach next summer, swim way out, maybe see Shamu …" he laughed.

Only ten minutes into this date seemed endless. He put his arm around me (heavy, like concrete and annoying) and smirked.

"Bet I can make a Mets fan out of you," he said slyly. I shuddered.

"Bet you can't," I told him. My family was generations of Yankee fans, proud ones. I was fine with that and would die a Yankees fan, you betcha. Besides, Mike wouldn't be in my life too much longer. His nose twitched and I stifled a giggle. Bet he stored little bugs in there all summer long.

"Mike, you know what? I'm getting a little tired or something," I said weakly. He was instantly gentle.

"Here, put your pretty little head right here, on Mike's big shoulder," he said. I felt out of place and clammy. Swallowing, up came acid reflux.

"I'd like us to visit again," he said when he brought me home.

"I don't think so, Mike. But thank you for a nice time," I told him. He sniffed and what a powerful noise *that* was.

"Yeah, good luck. Maybe you'll marry a Yankee," he said the word Yankee as though it tasted bitter in his mouth.

I laughed. That would be quite nice, I thought. He gave me the incentive to get Yankee tickets for my sister and me the following week. You never know who you might meet at Yankee Stadium. Definitely not Mike.

Big Bad Matthew

The initial telephone conversation with Matthew was impressive-he owned two large sporting goods stores in New York. A third was opening 'soon' in Connecticut and a fourth was in the planning stages. He had a Master's degree in business management, had traveled the world and had much to offer, so he said.

"Never call me Matt, though," he warned ominously. I shrugged and made a face into the telephone.

"You can call me Tessa, then, not Tess," I responded.

"How about if I call you for Saturday night?" Said Matthew.

He scored on that one, figuratively speaking. His deep throaty voice would have been sensual if it wasn't followed by hard sighs. A self-impressed voice; used to giving orders. Matthew liked the fact that I was independent, childless and involved in organizations. He detested weak, cloying women, mentioned having a son somewhere and was vague about being free now in his pursuits. He had tickets for a show and would I accompany him? Absolutely. Yes, Matthew.

He arrived twenty minutes early. Matthew was huge, more than 100 pounds overweight. He actually lumbered up my twelve apartment steps and panted. His sport jacket was a beautiful shade of green and his face was a scary shade of red. I gave him some water and had him sit down immediately. For the thousandth time I asked: Why me?

When I re-entered the living room, he was engrossed in a cooking channel but looked me up and down.

"Hey, purple suits you doll, you're all right. Ready?" He struggled to get up from the deep-cushioned couch. I gave him my hand and kind of jerked him to his feet. He gave me a quick peck on the cheek. His cologne was expensive.

Out to his car (Volvo, loaded) we went. He made a phone call, mumbling business, and apologized.

"Sorry, doll, work, work, work. They can't function ... yeah, Bill?" and he chatted with "Bill" about nonsense. I toyed with the radio, powdered my nose and tried not to look as annoyed as I felt. Matthew's heavy breathing reminded me of Darth Vader's and made me nervous. He drove into New York City with the ease of someone who commutes every day. He cut people off, chewed mints, breathed hard and was generally annoying. He offered me mints, "not 'cause you need 'em, doll, but Mom said to share," and I took two just to have something to do. I hoped the play would be lengthy; too much free time with this character would be unbearable.

When the theater lights darkened, Matthew's breathing sounded *loud*. The stranger on his other side threw him looks of disdain but Matthew remained blissfully unaware. When the couple on stage sang a love song, Darth put his hand on my knee. And it began to travel. Idiot. I quietly (but firmly) removed his hand from my leg. The stranger chuckled. Matthew seemed to gasp.

"Ok, I'll wait till later," he whispered into my ear. Oh, boy, I had my work cut out for me. It was likely that this boy expected 'reimbursement' for his treating me to this outing. No sirree, I said to myself, I'm not bending any rules for Buddha here.

After the play, Matthew and I ventured into Greenwich Village, where people of all sizes, races and types strolled leisurely. Here, Matthew seemed less obese. We went to a lovely Italian restaurant where my date called the waitress "Toots." She rolled her eyes and mouthed "You poor thing" to me.

The food was excellent, we chatted, but I was on guard. They cleaned off our table and my mammoth date had the nerve to touch my leg-again-under the table.

"Stop that," I hissed.

"Ooh, you're a feisty one. Good, I like that ..." He licked his lips.

"Matthew, I hope you understand ... I'm not that kind of woman...."

"Don't say a word, doll-baby. I know all about you," he grinned. He was despicable. I belched (silently) spaghetti sauce laced with disgust.

We walked to his car and I gently explained that I don't become physical on dates, if you know what I mean, Matthew.

"Tessa, I like you. I wanna touch you all over, give me a chance to make you a happy woman, I know things … good things," he said and his voice dripped with oil and heaviness.

"I'm flattered, really. But, no, no thank you. It's not my style. Gosh, this is just our first date," I whispered.

"Yeah, yeah," he muttered. "Guess you have your reasons. A prude I had to pick. A prude and a teaser to boot. Still, you turn me on, Tessa, you just do," and his shoulders moved with every labored breath.

"I'm sorry, Matt. I mean, Matthew. But no."

He shook his head and I saw the sweat glistening on his forehead. It was not a pretty sight. He drove silently back into New Jersey. When the streets became familiar, I relaxed. He smiled and began to massage my shoulder.

"Is the little girl happier at home maybe? Should Daddy come in and take care of his little pet?" he asked. I worked hard not to puke in the Volvo.

"Thanks anyway, but no. I think we had a lovely evening, and I would just like to say good night right here, in your car. Thank you Matthew." I extended my hand. He pulled me toward him and attempted to hug me but I was quicker. And healthier.

"Matthew, decent women don't like this type of thing. Get a life!" And I high-tailed it from his car, slamming the door with a vengeance. I got my keys, and bolted into the safety of my home. His car started back up and then it was gone. I breathed. My heavy sigh sounded like him … time for tea, a long shower, and a good book. I heated up the teapot and stared into space.

Two months later I read Matthew's obituary in the local newspaper. He suffered a fatal heart attack at work. I did not grieve. Women everywhere were safer.

Women-Speak

Dana, Sarah, Mary Beth and I met for an early supper. Mary Beth had an announcement:

"I am definitely leaving Greg," she tells us. She tells us this every few months. We roll our eyes, we shake our heads. We know our friend and her addiction to Greg, married man who swears he loves her.

"He's not going to leave Lois," she says.

He never was going to leave Lois. Or marry Mary Beth or give her children or move with her to Vermont. Mary Beth has refused to see what everyone else always did. Until now.

"I can't believe he's just going to stay with her. She's so demanding!"

And I can't believe we are all patiently listening to this diatribe once again.

"Mary Beth, what's changed?" I say, wanting to scream at her.

"Well, he ... he, well, he's having another baby. Do you believe that? It was an accident, he said. An accident! He told me they hadn't been together in years, so how can that be?" Her face crumpled like old tissues.

How can it be, that someone so intelligent and realistic could be so dumb and blind about a relationship, I wondered. I know there are so many books on this topic. But Mary Beth is my friend and after four years of this crazy relationship (including a brief time where they ran away to see foliage in Vermont and he promised to move there with her after ... but after never comes) I was tired of her opting not to see the truth. She simply did not want to.

"So ... are you sure this time? It's getting pretty monotonous and you aren't getting any younger, you know," said Sarah pointedly.

"No, this time is different," says Mary Beth. "He lied."

This time he lied? What about all the lies for all the years? He has been lying to his family about his whereabouts, to his employer when he takes off for long, mysterious lunches, to his colleagues ... he has done nothing but lie. I shake my head and blow angry bangs off my forehead.

"I'm glad. I have missed you so much," says Dana and hugs Mary Beth hard. Dana is one of those women there are too few of-she doesn't give in to judgmental feelings. If you are hurting or joyful, she simply shares your heart with you and is there for you. Most of the time, I am too annoyed to be like Dana. But right now, she made Mary Beth smile and that is worth something to all of us.

"He said he hopes the baby will make Lois happy because he never could," says Mary Beth. I can't stand it.

"He made her happy at least three times that we know of," I say with an edge. "And it's you he's made miserable. Wait, I'm wrong. You make yourself miserable, and I hope you are done with this already!" I stand up and take deep breaths so I don't haul off and hit someone.

"Calm down, Tessa. This is her life, not yours," says Sarah. "She's trying to make a change. We need to support her."

"Support her? We have been listening to this for years ... through the other new babies, through his mid-life crisis, through his surgeries, his jobs ... I feel like he's another case in my files" I hear my voice, sharp and unforgiving.

"Tessa, we listen to your dating stories, your brother's problems, your life, don't we?" said Dana ever-so-gently. I look at my shoes and feel warm. Have I become less of a friend? I didn't think so.

"The truth is, Mary Beth, we've gone through this a gazillion times with you," admits Sarah. I silently thank her for being on my side.

"I know, I know," says Mary Beth with wet eyes. "But I love him, and I'm afraid I will always love him. Then what will I do?" And she covers her eyes.

"You will get older, you will move on, you will be our friend and you will eat enormous amounts of chocolate marshmallow ice cream." I tell her. She lifts up her face and smiles in spite of the sadness.

"Thanks Tessa. I know you're tired of hearing it. But I want to be done with him, really. I just don't know how." I grab her hand and squeeze it. We are in this together, this battle to make it right with someone.

"You tell him you met someone else. You meet his eyes, and you sit up straight. You tell him you didn't realize he doesn't meet your needs. You tell him you've been lying to yourself. And you walk away."

She looks horrified. "You mean, lie?"

"YES," we all say in unison. She looks like she might be sick.

"Yeah, maybe," she says and we look at each other. Mary Beth doesn't convince any of us.

"Well, Tessa, what've you been up to?" asks Sarah. Truly, we need to change the subject.

"You mean you want to hear about my last date?" My friends perk up, even Mary Beth. So I amuse them with yet another story.

Kevin, About Kevin

When Kevin Ahlstrom called, his voice got my attention: throaty, musical and self-confident. He seemed totally comfortable calling and making small talk with a complete stranger which put me off somewhat.

"Kevin, what do you do in your spare time?" I asked.

"Is this a job interview?" He responded, testily I thought.

"Sorry. I didn't rehearse this, you know. OK, when you're not working as a drug company rep, what do you do? There, is that better?" I felt my growing annoyance.

"Yeah, that's good. Well, I like biking, travel, collecting shells, and eating ... amongst a lot of other stuff. Tess, let's meet and ask questions in person." He was right to the point for sure.

And so Kevin of the good voice and I of the great hair set a date. We met at a local park, on our bikes. I liked that idea; I could always bike away, far away, if necessary. It wasn't. He was handsome, tall and friendly. Friendly to every person who said hello or nodded. He talked without a stop, and even to an annoying duck in our path.

"Hey, quack-quack, look out, you're in our way. Ok, where was I? Oh yeah, about traveling to Paris ... beautiful country, great food, lots of free spirited people, ya know? Not all hung up, ya know? How ya doin' there, Tess? You look tired. Do I talk too much?"

I wondered if that was a rhetorical question and if I answered honestly, would he pedal away? Kevin was magnetized to his own verbiage. He liked to hear his voice more than I did. He hummed, talked, sang, whistled ... he was totally vocal. A psychiatrist might say he feared silences. I feared this bike ride was not going to end soon enough for me.

"Hey, Kev, I am tired. You go on ahead if you want ... I need some time off this thing. Maybe I'll hang out awhile."

He joined me. We parked the bikes and sat on rocks, overlooking a dirty pond with bread floating in it.

"See the ducks won't even eat that ... everyone feeds them, not me though. Not necessary. They need to find their own food. I saw a documentary-you like documentaries? They teach you a lot. Anyway, when we feed the wild birds, they rely on that instead of using their inherent skills, you know? "He breathed a second and I jumped in.

"Kevin, I feel like you don't know a thing about me ... aren't you going to ask me anything?"

"Nah," he instantly responded, "don't like to pry. But did I tell you about the Vatican? Went there in '83 ... it was fascinating, the city, all the protocol. I like order. You like order? Yeah, I go for that. Anyhoo, yeah, the Vatican, what a trip. Let's see, where else did I go? Oh, yeah ..."

I stood up. "Kevin, you're lecturing, not dating. Big difference, ya know?" He stared up at me with what I saw were very pretty eyes, light and filmy. Teary. Yikes, was he going to cry or something?

"Sorry, Tess. Lotsa folks can't keep up with me, I'm real fast-paced and I think a thousand thoughts a second. I just have done a lot, seen a lot, ya know? I'm kind of unusual you could say but I sure didn't mean to bore you. I'm just trying to share my life with someone, ya know?"

Indeed. Weren't we all trying to do just that? But I had learned something he apparently did not: sharing means give and take, back and forth. He was all one-dimensional. I got on my bike and actually blew him a fake kiss in the air. "We're too different. Nice, but different," and I rode away. He stayed on the rock, but I heard his voice again shortly.

"Hey quack-quack, don't eat the bread ... go for insects or something. It's not really good for ya ..."

Now, back home, eating a bowl of Cheerios and phoning my friend Regina, I was safe. There are so many, entirely too many, weird dates out there. I think that in just a few months, Kevin will have permanent laryngitis. He used up all the speech he was intended to spread out over a lifetime. And I don't think he will ever be too lonely. There is always a creature to speak to but lucky for ducks, they can simply flap once and escape into the air, leaving the talking machine to himself.

"Hi Regina, I really need to talk."

Singles Dance (Sometimes)

In between these dates, Sara and I sometimes work up the guts to go dancing. At least we intend to dance when we get there. Who knows?

It is inevitable. A short (very short, like approaching my shoulders) man with a shock of red hair stammers.

"Uh, uh, hi there. Wanna dance with me?"

No, I do not nor do I care to pet a porcupine. But the man is waiting.

"No thank you, I'm just relaxing right now," I tell him politely.

He raises his eyebrows in disapproval.

"Relax? C'mon, this is a d-a-n-c-e. You can relax later."

The man has tenacity, I give him that. But he obviously doesn't know I'm a former spelling bee champ.

"Thank you, but no," I am now firm. I could have said N-O but didn't want to lower myself. He didn't walk away rejected. He didn't seem disappointed. He stood there, staring. Sara was watching with that amusing little smile she saves for these moments.

"She's too tall for you," she tells him.

"That's dumb ... you can just dance, ya know? C'mon," He pulls my hand. I am going to use my outside voice now.

"LEAVE ME ALONE, RED. I AM NOT GOING TO DANCE WITH YOU, EVER."

His mouth drops and he shakes his head. He does not look embarrassed but does walk away. Sara's eyes are shut. "Did you have to scream?" She asks me.

"Yes, I did. Do you have a better solution?" She shakes her short pixie-like hair and the waves move independently. She is so adorable. Why do we have to go to these dances anyway?

A man with a plaid shirt and checked pants looks us over, up and down, and doesn't say a word. He has on two different socks. I stifle my giggle. He keeps checking us out and Sara stares at his feet.

"Are you stuck there?" She asks him.

He ambles away. "Do you have to be rude?" I ask, laughing.

The music plays a slow number, an oldie I like that brings me to a seventh grade dance. I see Pete Krause now, loose and lanky, choosing me from a group of girls, to dance with. It was so easy then. He is surely married now with kids and forgot all about me.

"Want to dance?" says the stranger. He is nice looking, a little nervous.

"Sure," I say as Sara nods approval. And so, we go out there and he leads, and breathes too heavily in my ear. He is dancing fairly well but he is too close to me and I am feeling as though I'm trapped in a hot car. I back up and he holds on. I am being anchored. The song is ending, thankfully, and he keeps dancing. Couples are moving off the floor, the music is changing and my partner, lead-like now, is leaning into me. I jerk away and he seems to wake up.

"Huh? Where ya goin?" He struggles with this big sentence and I simply blend into the crowd. Sara is dancing with someone and I go to get a glass of punch. Swallowing the cold citrus feels wonderful. I am amazed by the experiences each time we go dancing, and each time I think it will be different. And it is different yet always horrible.

"Hey, ya relaxed enough now?" Asks Red. I finish my punch in one gulp, shake my curly hair hard and leave. Sara joins me.

"Why do we do this?" she sounds about to cry.

Because, as she well knows, we are trying to meet a husband, a nice man with clothes that match, who knows how to socially interact with normalcy, who likes if not loves his mother and we are trying to find him as soon as possible.

"Janine met Bill at a dance," I offer, "and look how happy they are." I name the one and only couple I know who met in this arena.

"But that was eight years ago," Sara reminds me. "And here we are."

Not for long. We got our coats, almost tripped over Red, and went straight to the diner. Time for cheesecake or chocolate mousse, and no nonsense.

Sara deserved to meet a nice man who would like her hair, her wit and the fact that her parents lived far away. She is, like me, so tired of dating. She dreams of someone she has named "Fred," who will be swept off his feet, marry her and present her with perfect children and a condo near the beach. She actually believes this will happen. But not tonight.

Tonight she is tired of dancing with strange men and waiting for "Fred." So we sip our decaf, eat our goodies slowly and nod, knowingly, at the other many single girls in the diner. We are all sharing the dream: walking away from this and to the altar where the "Fred's" of our futures are waiting.

Teddy and I Going Nowhere

There are dates that baffle: why could we not have made it work? The answer isn't simple and sometimes there simply is no answer. Such was Teddy.

He picked me up in an old Mustang, a cool car indeed. He was slightly taller than I, lean, kind of athletic, with a bounce to his walk. He said, "How do?" when we met, which I found refreshing.

To go to the off-Broadway musical, I dressed a little funky in a peasant blouse, wrap around skirt, and sandals. I looked like a Bible character and he resembled a short basketball player.

Teddy had weird teeth-they seemed to slant forward and gave him a sort of camel-mouth look. He wore unrecognizable cologne, from which I got a slight headache. We were not too impressed with one another but both very polite. The evening began stiffly and conversation was more awkward than I recalled when we spoke on the phone.

"So, Teddy, do you go to New York often?" I began.

"Yeah, sometimes. You?"

"Yeah, occasionally."

Not too thrilling yet. I folded my hands on my lap, and I felt his glance.

"Are you praying?" He asked.

"No, just sitting." Praying in the car? Here we go again, I thought. Weird stuff.

"Do you sew or anything?" He asked. I shook my head. I had never been asked that question except by a home economics teacher.

"Well, what do you do?" He asked with a tone of impatience.

"A lot. I read, go to plays, take courses, lots of different things. You?"

He sighed. I could not be sure if the sigh meant boredom or something worse-no answer.

"Tessa, I have to concentrate on the road right now. Give me a minute."

I looked around. There was barely any traffic, and the ride didn't seem nerve-wracking to me, except for the attitude of the driver. I wished I was at Baskin Robbins with any female friend I had. I even wished I was home alone.

Teddy and I watched the show, laughed a bit, and he asked me if I wanted to "extend the evening." It was a nice attempt but no, I had hoped to shorten it actually.

"Teddy, we aren't connecting for some reason," I said.

"Yeah, I know. Why is that?"

I wasn't sure. I didn't like his driving, his scent or his mouth, for starters.

"You know, maybe we're just two nice people made for two other people," he offered. That was not Teddy's original thought but it worked.

"Yeah, maybe," I agreed.

So I got home, stared into the mirror, and wondered why he didn't try harder to "extend the evening." I could not see any reason at all. Maybe the chemistry wasn't there, maybe he liked quieter women, and maybe he was dead on about us being right for two other people.

I would like to know where those other people are before I age too much further. I quit thinking about it as I delved into the freezer where my good friend, Cherry Garcia, made known his presence. And the dating, like the beat, goes on.

An Attorney at his Game

Marcus and I got together after one phone conversation, which left me overly eager. He sounded so ... organized. He was divorced with two children he saw weekends, and also liked racquetball, nice restaurants and fresh air. In fact, he belonged to a hiking club out of western New York State, and invited me to join him and his group on a Sunday afternoon. (He said his kids were visiting their Grandma in Massachusetts). His work fascinated him: he had been a legal aid attorney and now worked in corporate law.

"It's less personal but more lucrative. Life is a trade-off, right?"

Right indeed. I had often thought of attorneys as self-centered and pompous but Marcus (I really liked that name) sounded very sweet and even nervous about meeting me. He said dates made him uptight. We were already sharing.

Marcus and I met at the hiking trail entrance, in a village named Apple-town and he assured me this was a beginner's hike. The leaves were turning color and the bright blue sky made the day ideal. Many hikers were friendly toward us and people shared trail mix and bottled water. A few leaned on walking sticks that reminded me of Moses. The older people seemed to have more stamina than the 30-something crowd, and I found out that walking briskly and conversing were impossible for me. Marcus was accommodating, and although I was sure he could walk at a very swift pace, he stayed with me, pointing out apple trees, scenic overlooks and wild flowers. It was a lovely day, culminating with everyone going out for apple cider and pie in a small country inn. One hiker asked Marcus where "Sheryl" was, and Marcus blanched-then smoothly said she wasn't around these days. I was busting with curiosity and hoped "Sheryl" had moved far away, like to Oregon. I didn't ask and Marcus didn't tell.

Two weeks later we had a late lunch at a restaurant where the waiters dressed in costume. Was it dumb luck that our waitress was dressed as a bride? I admired her veil, her beading and the look of regal beauty that seems to enjoin girls on their special day. Marcus hummed 'Here comes the bride," and I silently began to really like him. We had easy conversation, a delicious meal and I almost danced with anticipation of a new life with attorney Marcus.

In the ladies room, alone, I winked at me in the mirror and saw myself look very happy and even a little smug. This might be the end of dates forever. I refreshed my lipstick and cologne, and sang "Going to the chapel." Shame on me for being so hopeful.

Marcus had said he lived near the restaurant-why then was he walking toward my car? I felt a stab of insecurity. I should have.

"Tessa, you are one very nice, very pretty lady," he said quietly. I waited for the but.

"I have to tell you … I live with someone, I'm not really single." He sounded depressed. Not half as much as I was at this minute.

"Sheryl, right?"

"Yeah. We haven't been getting along too well, and I thought …"

"You thought you would cheat on her and try me out. Real nice, Marcus," I sounded bitter. Good, he deserved it. Through blurry eyes, I spotted my car.

"Tessa, I know it sounds bad but honestly, I want to break it off …"

I shook my head. I wasn't forgiving him.

"Marcus, you break off and then you go on dates. This isn't fair to me or her, and it's kind of beneath all of us, don't you think?" I stared at his green eyes, realizing right then how betrayed I felt. And missing him already.

On the drive home, I felt chills and decided he had made me catch a cold. This dating ritual was beginning to wear me out. I was eager to see my little apartment with its familiar presence and welcoming candles. I would make tea and call Dana, and probably cry later. I thought of Marcus leaving his house to meet me (and maybe many others), getting our hopes up falsely. We should all get together and file a class action lawsuit!

I half-grinned at the scenario, and decided one thing: I was very glad not to be Sheryl.

Maybe I would adopt a parakeet and just stay home with it. Budgie and me, true love, forever. It might be boring at times, but not so hard on my heart. I suddenly wished for a crazy life like my ex has, with a wife, animals, kids, noise … sounded very warm and cozy.

"Hi, Dana? I am so depressed. He lives with someone. I'm thinking of getting a bird." The sound of my friend's voice and compassion made me burst into tears, and I knew I didn't want a parakeet; I simply wanted something pretty and fun to take my mind off the Marcus's of my life.

I thought, too, it might be nice to have wings and fly away when you just can't take it anymore.

And So It Goes

I, Tessa, do hereby resolve ... oh, forget it. I cannot resolve to stop dating because I have resolved to find a future with someone. Is this a big request? Seems to be.

Saw another "ex" recently, and he is extremely bitter, older, and paunchy. If I don't meet someone soon, I will also be older (never bitter, not heavier, please God). Neil was a mamma's boy, but mamma died, and he cannot replace her. What woman today will bother making homemade everything and keeping a kosher home? Well, there are some, but Neil doesn't want to find an Orthodox Jewish girl, he wants a modern Millie who takes off 'modern' in the kitchen. Doesn't happen, Neil. I empathized with his loneliness and fought back tears as I recalled our one year together when we dated and started to make some plans. Before long though, those plans got scrapped. Neil had issues in his past he hadn't bothered to share: issues of chronic pain, two hospitalizations for back ailments, and agoraphobia. I could not imagine having kids with such a man, because raising kids takes well adjusted parents. His therapist, a nervous wreck who habitually twisted the hair on her head forming stiff ringlets, told me flat out, "Neil is a very sick man and you are a young woman. You decide if this is something you want to be part of." I decided when I exited the office that I had to move along, leaving Neil to hopefully find a more qualified therapist ... and a more committed girlfriend. After marrying (and divorcing, so predictable) Neil called me to say he was "fine" and did I want to meet for dinner? He wasn't fine enough for this girl, and no, dinner would not be an option. I had heard (from a good reliable source, his sister's best friend) he'd moved to the Los Angeles area, had an affair with a Mexican woman and fathered two sons with her. This he failed to mention. I am so done with Neil.

But what to do? A friend has asked me to accompany her to a rural area of Pennsylvania, where patriotic-type Americans have street fairs, parades, and county 4-H competitions. I am going. This will be a chance to get away from my life here-the career that bends my heartstrings out of alignment, the lack of suitable partners, the constant visiting of diners for late-night snacks (because the date was so awful)—all of it. I need a break. Surely I will not focus on meeting a man in that environment and a weekend away is just the remedy for the blues of this sort. I am tired, so tired, of the dating routine, the pressure. I am anticipating silliness, well-groomed animals, homemade jelly and not seeing anyone I know for miles when we take this ride away, my lady friend and me. It is exactly what I need.

Fast forward. The weekend away was terrific. There was so much beauty in the western Pennsylvania mountains. The county fair was just like in the movies. I petted calves, bought blackberry jam, spoke with real farmers and their families, and photographed covered bridges (like in the movie with Meryl Streep). It was blissful.

And I met a man.

He is far away now, but he calls me. He lives alone, he and his beagle, Beau, and something stirred in both of us. Who knows what will be? I continue to work with children and volunteer in the community, but dream of this man and hold out a hope that if it's meant to be, it will work out. As I cook, clean and do laundry, I think of his house, his dog, our time together taking pictures and sharing a few kisses. As I attended a coworker's retirement dinner, I teased myself into thinking I am the hon-ored guest, the one leaving. It is a dream, a hope, maybe this time. Mom said "sometimes you meet a man when you're not even looking" and so, I hope, because I truly wasn't looking.

I peer out my tiny bedroom window and see the clouds pulling in, the night drawing closer. In that now far—away country area, millions of stars came out one night, twinkling and looking like the planetarium in New York City. And the smell ... sweet hay, clean air, fields of wild flowers, it was breathtaking. So was he. Lanky, quiet, a gentleman.

I want to see it all again. Him too, I know he's a part of it. Maybe this time …

Tessa's Epilogue

I gently finger this journal. Tears form in my eyes as I recall, in vivid detail, each of these experiences. I can laugh now too, especially at Meow Man as I gaze at the big ball of calico fur in my lap. The sunlight filters through the mini-blinds onto her many colors and I resist the urge to squeeze her out of sheer joy. I feel the chill on the bridge that day with Tony, and wonder if he is still beseeching his dead brother to visit him. He might have enjoyed some comfort from a pet rather than to try mixing with the deceased. I hear a little snore and see Candi, our small Tibetan dog sleeping. They all sleep like that, her groomer said, with their necks twisted like a pretzel and their paws seemingly in prayer. She is dreaming. Her ears twitch and she growls a little. I smile at the simplicity of my creatures, which always choose to be within two feet of my presence. The office room I am in dances with sunlight and warm hues. The aroma of cinnamon tea permeates my favorite haunt in this house. I peruse further. I look through college pictures, newsletters I'd written, and poetry I sweated over. There are term papers in an old satchel and a picture of a former pen pal from Israel. He and I had exchanged photographs and when he said I was pretty but American girls were too heavy, I never wrote back. Painful memories, even now. The dog awakens.

"Hey, sweetie," I coo and rub her belly. She lolls about, as the cat gives us both injured looks and tries to slit her eyes against this vision of jealousy. "I have enough love for both of you, now." I tell her.

For all of us. Yes, there's a husband. The one from the rural country-did you guess that part? He was THE ONE, just like Mom said; the one I'd find when I wasn't looking. (Except deep down we're always looking).

And I got the house, the pets, and the life I envisioned. Minus the children; we were too middle-aged for that dream. You can not have it all, but you can have most of it.

"Look, Candi," I pointed, "this was Jeremiah. He turned out to be gay but gave me his picture because he knew, just knew, he would be famous someday. We went to dinner and he asked me if I had any brothers or close guy-friends, gay ones. He was very funny but I guess I don't need this picture, huh pup-pup?" The little dog ran and brought me her favorite toy, a hard green plastic bone. I threw Green Bone across the room and ripped up Jeremiah.

The cat stirs from slumber and stretches her two front paws way out in front of her. She is entertaining when she least tries. She is magical and curious, always looking around the bend for one more adventure. She breathes with her entire cat-body and her long fur ripples slightly. There is untold joy in watching one's pets and reading old letters.

I have come to know some things: Never give up hope. Walk or run away from any person who makes you uncomfortable. Laugh hard, every day. Pray for even the small things and praise God for all things. Don't sit still too long. Don't believe everything you hear.

But believe this: you are worthy in this world and you must give your time and talents to others. Love your pets and learn about loyalty. Don't date anyone who ever hit a woman (for any reason). Let others speak of your virtues and volunteer your time. Use moisturizer.

You were born for a reason and you are supposed to share that reason with someone. Go forward and find him and make the world better by being a couple. Ah, love.

Printed in the United States
214574BV00001B/9/P